Please don't cry. I don't want your
book to get stained with tears.
Anyway, it's not so bad.

Amy is a piece
of sweetcorn.

Amy had been looking forward to this moment all her life. It was as exciting as five birthdays and eight Christmases rolled into one.

"WooHooo!"
said Amy.

Noah didn't **just** eat Amy.

One piece of sweetcorn isn't enough for dinner – unless you're a large fly or a small mouse. But Noah isn't a large fly or a small mouse. He's a medium-sized boy.

ADAM KAY & HENRY PAKER

PUFFIN

This is the story of Noah and Amy. Say hi to Noah.

Say hi to Amy.

Oh, you can't. Noah's just eaten her.

Noah's dinner was a nice glass of **milk**,
and a slice of pizza with . . .

cheese,

and **tomato**,

and **lime**,

and **egg**,

and **onion**,

and **raisin**

and . . . **Amy**.

Hey, don't judge him. We all like
different things on our pizzas.

"Hooray! I love adventures!" said Tomato.

"**WHEEE!!**" said Amy.

She **SWOOSHED** to the left

and **SWISHED** to the right,

GULP!

Noah swallowed everything that was in his mouth, and Amy zoomed down his throat like she was on the world's best waterslide.

THIS WAY

KAY'S ANATOMY

ALICE IN
WONDERLAND

she *looped* the loop

and **SPUN** like
a spinning top.

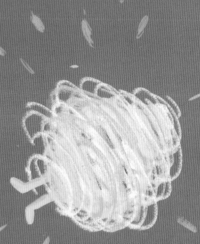

KEEP
GOING →

DONK!

"Wow! What is this place?" asked Amy.

"This is Noah's stomach," said a wise old raisin.

Amy noticed the baked bean sandwich Noah had eaten for breakfast.

Hey, don't judge him. We all like different things in our sandwiches.

Then she saw the chocolate cake and ketchup Noah had eaten for lunch. (OK, you can judge him for that.)

Amy had just spotted her other friends from the pizza when suddenly . . .

. . . everything started **shaking**.

There was an extremely loud noise, and everyone covered their ears.

BURP!!

"Noah is always doing that," said the Wise Old Raisin.

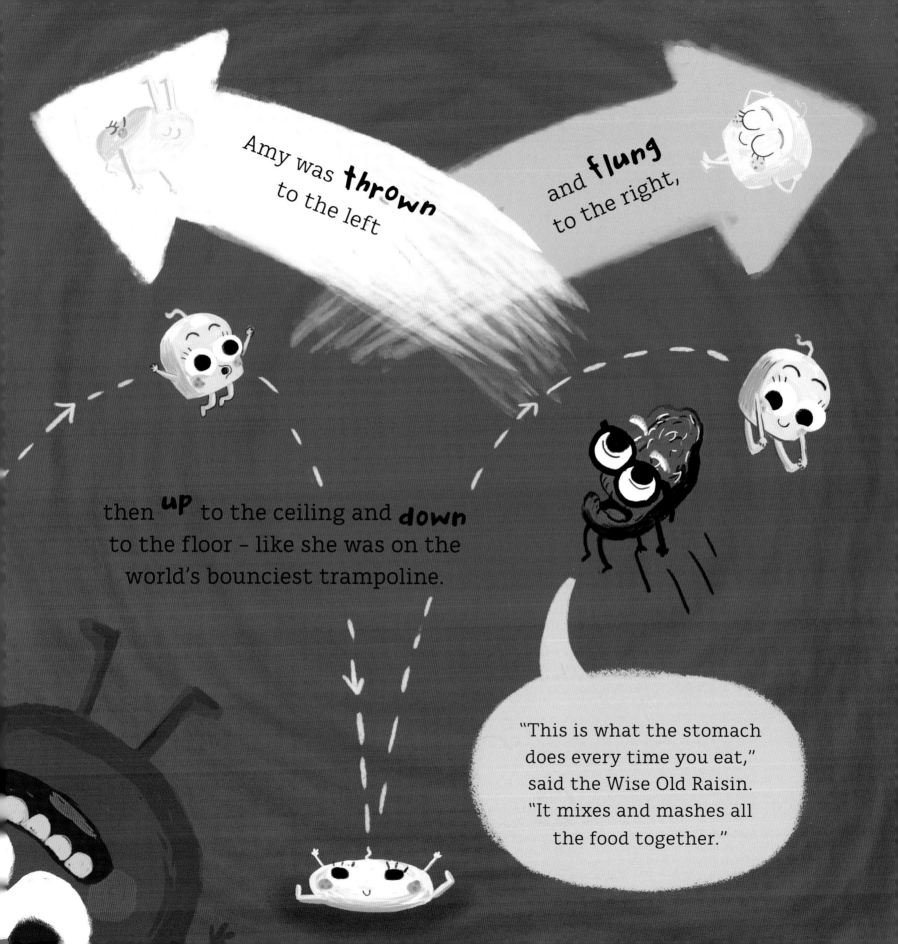

Amy was **thrown** to the left and **flung** to the right,

then **up** to the ceiling and **down** to the floor – like she was on the world's bounciest trampoline.

"This is what the stomach does every time you eat," said the Wise Old Raisin. "It mixes and mashes all the food together."

Noah's stomach started to fill up with liquid.

And then.... WHOOSH!

Everything slurped out of the stomach

and into a tunnel called the

SMALL
INTESTINE.

Amy kept going.

And going.

Amy saw bits of food getting squashed through the walls.

Then Amy was swept down a brown river
into an even **bigger** tunnel.

"Hello?"
said Amy.

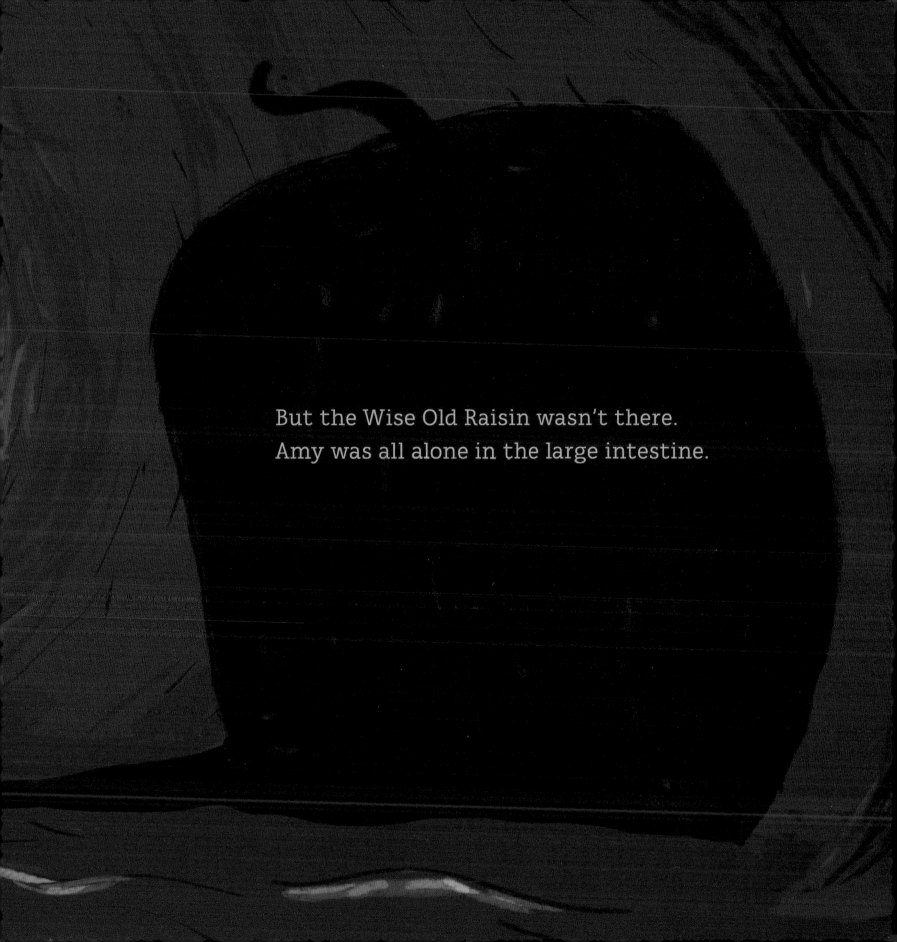

But the Wise Old Raisin wasn't there.
Amy was all alone in the large intestine.

The brown river carried Amy
on, all by herself. It was a bit
dark and a bit scary.

Suddenly, all the water got
squeezed out of the river,
turning it from a brown
liquid into a brown lump.

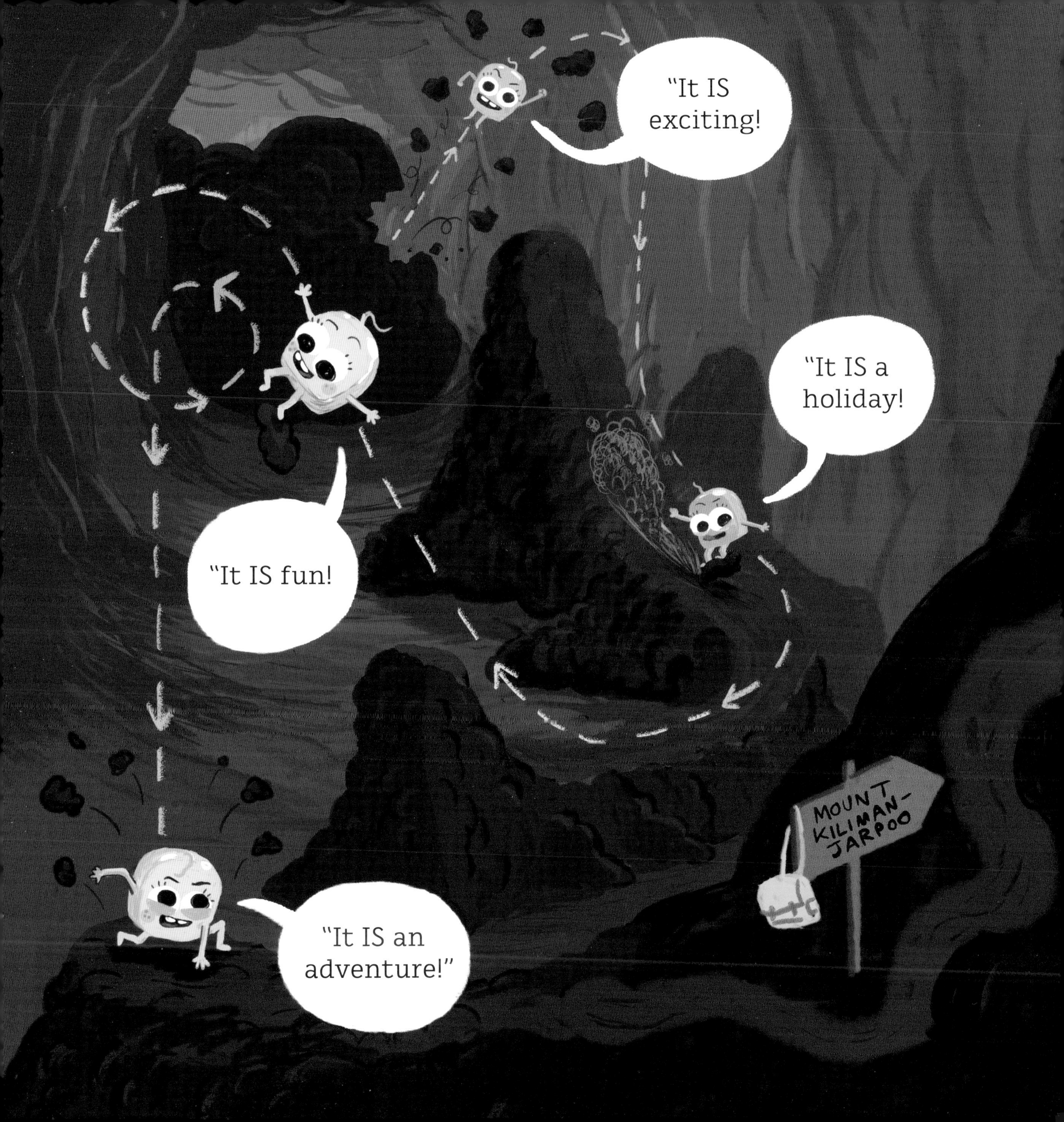
"It IS exciting!
"It IS fun!
"It IS a holiday!
"It IS an adventure!"
MOUNT KILIMAN-JARPOO

Noah went to the bathroom, sat on the toilet, and there was a loud

SPLASH!

Amy and the poo **squeezed** out of Noah's bottom.

Noah looked down
into the toilet bowl.

"I wonder how that
piece of sweetcorn got
in there?" said Noah.

He flushed the toilet, and Amy disappeared down into the pipe.

To poos everywhere. And Ruby, I guess – Adam

To Margot, Audrey and Sophie – Henry

PUFFIN BOOKS

UK | USA | Canada | Ireland | Australia | India | New Zealand | South Africa

Puffin Books is part of the Penguin Random House group of companies whose
addresses can be found at global.penguinrandomhouse.com.

Penguin
Random House
UK

First published 2023
001
Text copyright © Adam Kay, 2023
Illustrations copyright © Henry Paker, 2023
The moral right of the author and illustrator has been asserted
Printed in Italy
The authorized representative in the EEA is Penguin Random House Ireland,
Morrison Chambers, 32 Nassau Street, Dublin D02 YH68
A CIP catalogue record for this book is available from the British Library
ISBN: 978–0–241–58590–0
All correspondence to: Puffin Books, Penguin Random House Children's
One Embassy Gardens, 8 Viaduct Gardens, London SW11 7BW

MIX
Paper from
responsible sources
FSC
www.fsc.org   FSC® C018179